Get Off the
Struggle Bus

WHAT READERS ARE SAYING ...

||||||||||||||||||||||||||||||||||||||||||||||||||||||||||||||||||||||||||||||

Get off the Struggle Bus is a book that needed to be written. Since being introduced to Shelley Pierce she has been an encourager, role model and a great friend. She has a way with writing that is honest, to the point and effectively shows the love that God has for everyone. *Get Off the Struggle Bus* is no exception. It is a book that I will keep on the shelf and give to all students who are going through the struggles of life!
—**Ross Turner**, Student Pastor

Get off the Struggle Bus is one of the most exciting books for children I have read. The combination of storyline and biblical teaching is truly groundbreaking. Shelley Pierce's use of word pictures to capture the thoughts, feelings, and emotions of young Sam will connect with children and make this book instantly relatable to them. I hope to use this wonderful book in my own ministry as we instruct children in not only the names of God, but how those names relate to who He is and how He relates to children in their lives. I have known Shelley for many years and know that she has an amazing heart for children and their families, helping them in their spiritual journey. This book will be a great addition to every family's devotion time or children's personal devotion. I encourage every parent to encourage their child to read *Get Off the Struggle Bus* either as a personal devotional book or as a family study.
—**Tim Thompson**, Children's Pastor

Shelley Pierce eloquently writes about real life for children and practical application of God's word. What amazing stories for children to learn the names of God and to strengthen their relationship with Him in their everyday life. This book helps children grow in their relationship with Christ and to see him for who he is and how he protects and provides for them. I highly recommend this book for all age groups. Sometimes even adults need to be reminded of such.
—**Diann Musgrove**, 7th grade teacher

I absolutely love the concept of this book! As a teen who has moved and lost a love one, I think that Sam is relatable. I do believe that there are a lot of teens who were born and raised in church that do not really understand that there are many names for God. I think that this book, (and I assume more to come), will provide a better understanding of God and His love for us. The way that Mrs. Shelley presents the different names for God will have a powerful impact on people's perspective of God.
—**Tori**, 7th Grade

I think it is amazing the way Mrs. Shelley conveyed God's all-powerfulness! As one who has moved a few times, I can relate to Sam on how sometimes it takes time to settle in to a new place. I genuinely believe this can bring a peace to those who are in Sam's similar situation. I also enjoyed how she also showed we need to pray for those who hurt and persecute us.
—**Jaida**, 10th Grade

I can't think of a better companion to the Bible in understanding the completeness of God than this book. It's a story and a workbook rolled into one; for any age.
—**Cari Walker**, Trail Life USA Volunteer

I've heard it said that the heart can't love what the mind doesn't know. I believe that's one of the reasons that God has led Shelley to write this book. She has found a beautiful way to weave His names and character into stories that are understandable for young readers. I am excited to have this resource available for families and church leaders to use in helping to fulfil the first and greatest commandment given by Jesus in scripture: "love the Lord your God with all your heart and with all your soul and with all your mind."
—**Sonya Higgs**, Manager, Christian Book & Gift Shop, Greeneville, TN

A Pastor friend of mine once told me: "Go ahead and yell. God's a big ol' boy! He can take it." This book does the same, minus the yell, for kids who are in the midst of problems, either external or internal, showing them how to talk to God in all of his characteristics. Any child, or adult, can use advice on how God comforts and supports us through all of our problems. Biblical and explained in a way that will make sense to a searching child, Shelley has hit the mark on this one.
—**Jeff Brigman**

Reading is not my favorite pastime but I could not stop reading this book! I felt like Sam's dad gave the book to me so I could discover God all over again. I found myself taking notes and digging deeper into my Bible to learn more. I giggled and cried but most of all I felt God.
—**Susan Beddingfield**

Wow! Wow! Wow! I am so touched by Shelley's writing. I would have loved to have had this book for my girls as they were growing up. God encouraged me as I read to continue to be intentional with my adult kids. I can think back on times this resource would have really helped me, as a mom,

to guide my girls to focus on God and what he wants for our lives. I highly recommend *Get Off the Struggle Bus*.
—Angie Mosley, Teacher, 4th Grade

Get Off the Struggle Bus

Shelley Pierce

ELK LAKE PUBLISHING INC
PUBLISHING THE POSITIVE
Plymouth, Massachusetts

Cover and Interior Design: Derinda Babcock

Editor(s): Derinda Babcock, Deb Haggerty

PUBLISHED BY: Elk Lake Publishing, Inc., 35 Dogwood Dr., Plymouth, MA 02360, 2021

Library Cataloging Data

Names: Pierce, Shelley (Shelley Pierce)

Get Off the Struggle Bus / Shelley Pierce

102 p. xx 15 cm × 23 cm (6 in × 9 in.)

ISBN-13: 978-1-64949-155-8 (paperback) | 978-1-64949-156-5 (trade paperback) | 978-1-64949-157-2 (e-book)

Key Words: Middle Grade, Names of God, Relocation, Family, Illness, Values & Virtues, Bible Study

Library of Congress Control Number: 2021933796 Fiction

DEDICATION

IIIIIIIIIIIIIIIIIIIIIIIIIIIIIIIIIIIIIIIII

To the children who struggle under the weight of life and need to know El Shaddai, God Almighty, who is truly the God of More than Enough.

And to the adults who struggle because they have yet to reach out to Elohim and take hold of our Creator and Sustainer's hand

NOTE

||||||||||||||

Sam is a fictional character, experiencing the same difficulties you face—belonging, peace, friendships, purpose, and maybe just wanting to feel comfortable and have fun. Sam and his family have moved in the middle of the school year, taking him from the only home and school he's ever known to surroundings that make him feel like a visitor.

God revealed himself in the Old Testament through names with meanings that show his character. These names appear, in the Hebrew language, in specific places throughout Scriptures found in the Old Testament.

Sam's dad gives him a book to help Sam discover who God is through his special names. Sam learns he can trust God to help him get through challenging days. Although Sam is fictional, the names of God and the Scripture passages quoted to help you understand them are all fact.

My prayer for you is that you will know you are not alone. I pray you will know God is near and he loves you. God has a purpose for you.

So, grab a Bible and a notebook or journal, find a comfy spot, and begin your journey to knowing God better and loving him more. Pray before you read. Ask God to help you understand. He hears your prayers, and he will answer.

I'm excited about God's plan for your life.

Your friend,

Shelley

ACKNOWLEDGMENTS

IIIIIIIIIIIIIIIIIIIIIIIIIIIIIIIIIIIIIIIIIIIIIIIIIIIIIIII

Thank you, Deb Haggerty, and Elk Lake Publishing for your patience, godly guidance, and believing in this project. You are a gift to me in countless ways.

Words cannot express my gratitude for you, Derinda Babcock, and your high standard in editing and amazing creativity in cover art design. I'm letting the secret out—you've made me better by teaching me as you go.

I owe a lifetime of appreciation to my sweetheart, Tommy Pierce. You've taught me what it means to be a disciple of Christ by your steadfast commitment to him. During the most challenging moments of writing, you are my prayer support as well as my concordance, thesaurus, and dictionary. After forty years of togetherness, I love doing life with you!

CHAPTER ONE

||||||||||||||||||||||||||||||||||||

Safe.
Familiar.
Easy.
Towering trees stood in the front of his old school where the buses lined up. The aroma of lemons hung in the hallways, invisibly hovering above the shiny floors.

Odd.
Different.
Uncomfortable.
Here. Only shrubs and flowers lining the walkway. Sam could see the reflection in the shiny floor of the lockers lining the hall but the smell ... well, ... no lemons.

Sam inched into Room 121 and waited. Would there be an empty seat?

Mr. Lee welcomed Sam and pointed to a chair before starting class announcements. Sam's mind wandered back to his old school. He missed trees. And friends. And the scent of lemons.

His thoughts took him home. Ready to be finished with this school day, he knew he would settle into a familiar, comfy chair with a cold soda in one hand and a sandwich in the other.

And that is exactly what he did as soon as he got home.

"So? Tell me about your day." Mom followed him into the family room.

"Eh. No lemons."

"Lemons?"

"Never mind."

"Did you make any friends? Tell me about your teacher. What did you have for lunch?"

"Wow, Mom, too many questions. School was school, okay? Just school."

"No need to be so grumpy. I just want to hear about your day." Mom shrugged. "I went out today and found a new grocery store. I felt like a visitor though. You know, they don't put things in the same places the Red Owl store back home does. The bakery is where produce should be. The new store is going to take some getting used to."

I wonder if the store smelled like lemons.

Mom left the room and Sam munched his sandwich. He didn't like much about this new place, but a sandwich is good no matter where a guy lives.

Friday arrived, and the longest week of Sam's life ended. He planned to stay home all weekend in his favorite and familiar chair.

Dad got in the truck as Sam got off the bus.

"Where ya going?"

"Hardware store. I need a few things so I can fix the loose ceiling fan in the sunroom. Want to ride along?"

Sam piled in and tossed his backpack to the floorboard. He put the window down and closed his eyes as the afternoon breeze washed over his face. After a few minutes of silence, Sam turned toward his father. "Dad, did you ever move when you were a kid?"

"We moved once, in my fourth-grade year. I remember feeling excited about a new school. New friends. New experiences. Adventure!"

"Adventure? Seriously, Dad. That's not how I describe our move."

"Your day couldn't have been that bad, could it?"

"Day? Try week. Everything here is wrong. Like trying to make a puzzle piece fit where it doesn't belong."

"We knew moving in the middle of the year wouldn't be easy."

"I don't know how to act here. I hate everything about this new town."

"Give yourself time, Son. You'll see. Life will get better."

"I don't think the way you do. You always see the bright side. Even when there isn't one."

"Sam, I see the bright side because I have faith."

"Faith?"

"God never told us life would always be easy. When you know who God is, your faith in him grows stronger. You'll notice your perception changes when your faith grows."

"I know who God is. He created the world. He's the Savior. What does that have to do with school?"

"True enough, he is Creator and Savior. But did you know God has different names?"

"Huh?"

"Each name has a special meaning. If you learn his names and meanings, you will get to know God's character. To you, I am Dad. At work, I'm Mr. Hunter. My parents call me Jr, and my sisters call me Bub. And your mom, well, let's just say she calls me Sweetie-pie-honey-bunch."

"Gross."

Dad laughed. "Hang in there with me. When you begin to know God, you will understand he is Healer, Provider, Sustainer, All Powerful, Almighty ..."

"Yeah, well ..."

"God wants you to know him and trust him. When you do, you'll begin to have a different perspective of the tough days. How about if I help you learn some of God's names and what they mean?"

"Do I have a choice?"

CHAPTER TWO:
ELOHIM POWERFUL GOD, CREATOR AND SUSTAINER OF ALL THAT EXISTS

||||||||||||||||||||||||||||||||||||||||||||||||||||||||||||||||||||||||||||||||

Pronounced: el-o-HEEM[1]

"Mornin', Son, rise and shine!" Dad stood in the doorway, holding a cup of coffee in one hand and a piece of toast in the other.

Sam groaned, "What time is it?"

"Time to introduce you to Elohim."

"Elo-who?"

"Elohim, powerful God, creator and sustainer of all that exists[2]. Get dressed and meet me downstairs."

"Be right down," Sam forced himself out of bed and grabbed a pair of shorts and a T-shirt.

He shuffled into the kitchen and poured some orange juice.

Dad slid a book across the table.

"What's this?"

"This is how you are going to learn more about God."

"Seriously Dad? You want me to read on a

1   Names of God Chart, Rose Publishing, 2003

2   The Names of God, Ken Hemphill, Broadman and Holman, 2001, page fifteen.

Saturday? Can't you just tell me what I need to know?"

"The chapters are short. One chapter each Saturday. Come talk to me after you finish today's assignment."

"Assignment?" Sam grumbled. "Saturday school."

He grabbed a piece of toast, found his comfy favorite chair, and got started.

Genesis 1:1 introduces us to Elohim, powerful God, creator and sustainer of all that exists. The book of Genesis reveals God is the creator of the world. Through God's name, Elohim, we learn he sustains all he created. One example of how God sustains creation is the sun. The sun sets every evening and rises every morning. God is the one who put nature into motion. He told the sun what to do and the sun obeys. God is in charge. He owns everything.

We read in Genesis we are created in God's image. That doesn't mean when we look into a mirror we see what God would see if he looked into a mirror. To be created in his image means we are eternal. While our physical bodies do not live forever, our soul will never cease to exist. We have been created with the ability to choose good, to love each other, and to live with and love him forever. His image is what is on the inside.

Have you ever felt invisible? Overlooked? Unimportant? Thrown away?

Meet Elohim, the One who created you on purpose and with a purpose.

GRACE

Grace and Ashley had been friends since first grade. Athletic, pretty, and smart, Ashley excelled at everything she did. Everyone wanted to hang out with her. Sometimes Grace wondered why, because Ashley could also be mean. She enjoyed the attention everyone poured on her, and if another girl somehow did something, *anything* better than she, Ashley could be cruel.

Middle school brought the hopes a true friendship would form. Grace wanted, more than anything, to know she mattered to Ashley. Since they'd met years earlier, Grace didn't know from one day to the next if Ashley would act like a friend or a stranger.

The first period of the morning, Grace made a super-awesome shot in basketball during gym class. Minutes earlier, Ashley had uncharacteristically air-balled her shot. When Grace's shot swooshed through the net, all her friends cheered! Grace's confidence soared at her accomplishment.

Without warning, a basketball careened through the air and slammed Grace in the side of her head. The force of the hit knocked her off balance, and she fell to the floor. She sat up and looked around, only to see the eyes of everyone in the gym staring back at her. Seconds later, she heard laughter. Her cheeks grew from warm to red hot when she realized Ashley had thrown the ball. Grace had seen her treat lots of kids this way, but she never thought Ashley would turn on her too.

The next morning, Grace wore her favorite teal shirt with swirls of hot pink and gray. As she stepped off the bus she saw Ashley talking with a group of girls.

The girls laughed as Grace walked up, "What's so funny?"

"Oh, you wouldn't understand," Katelyn sneered, "you know, an inside joke."

"Yeah, and *you're* not inside." The hateful words flowed effortlessly through Ashley's perfectly pink glossed lips.

More laughter.

Ashley and the girls turned to walk away. Ashley didn't even try to speak quietly as she exclaimed, "Did you see that shirt? Wow. She must not have a mirror at her house."

Ashley's words stung like yellow jackets on the attack. Grace didn't quite know what to do. On a normal morning, she would be with the girls in the cafeteria grabbing breakfast before class.

I don't know why I thought I could hang out with Ashley and the girls. She's right, I'm an outsider."

The first volleyball practice of the season began at the end of the school day. Grace twisted her hands together as she sat down on the bench in the gym. She recalled the squeals and screams they shared when she and Ashley learned they both made the volleyball team. She wiped her clammy palms on the front of her T-shirt.

Their voices reached the gymnasium before the gaggle of girls ambled in. They sauntered right past her as if she didn't exist. No one even glanced her way. They followed Ashley to the top rung of the bleachers. The back of Grace's head burned as she could imagine the girls' taunting looks. Coach entered, and practice began. Grace worked hard to impress the coach during drills. All the while, no one spoke her name.

I don't know what I did to deserve this. I'm so alone.

Grace didn't say much when she got home.

That evening at bedtime, her mom knocked on her door.

"Yeah?"

"What's up? You usually tell me all the details of your day. Are you okay?"

"I'm tired, that's all. And ...well ... just ... Ashley." She kept her voice low but couldn't keep her words smooth.

"Oh, not again. I'm sorry Gracie, I so hoped this year would be different."

"This year *is* different. She's never been this mean to me. Mom, I think my friends threw me away."

Mom hugged Grace. "I think I can help you," she whispered. "Give me a few minutes. I'll be right back."

Grace wondered what her mom could possibly do or say to make her feel better.

Moments later, Mom returned and sat down on Grace's bed. "There have always been mean girls. Only God knows why Ashley treats you this way. I have two things I want you to do. First, read the Bible verses I've written down for you. Be sure you take your time. Second, begin to pray every day for Ashley, and ask God to help her know how precious she is to him."

Grace didn't really feel like reading the Bible right now. What good would Bible verses do? Reading seemed pointless, but she chose to listen to her Mom.

Mom had written a note above the verses:

Dear Grace,

God's name "Elohim" means "Powerful God, Creator and Sustainer of all that exists."

Long before he created the world, he knew you would be here at this moment, hurting and having this kind of day. He created you in an amazing way—after his very own image.

As you read these verses, I hope you will realize that Elohim knit you together just as Psalm 139 describes. He had a purpose for you and knew your name before you were born.

These verses will help you know Elohim also created Ashley. He loves each of you the same. I don't understand why she treats you as she does, but Elohim has a purpose for Ashley, too.

Just as sure as he created you, he will sustain you. That means he will give you what you need to stand strong on these hard days.

I love you Gracie, you can never be thrown away by anyone. Elohim, Powerful God, your Creator and Sustainer, created you on purpose and with a purpose!

Mom

Psalm 139   Jeremiah 29:11   Isaiah 40:31   James 1:2-8
Ephesians 3:14-18   Philippians 1:6

A tear fell to the note. Grace spent the next hour in her room reading the Bible verses and praying.

With each verse she read, the weight on her heart lifted. Best of all, she prayed and asked Elohim to watch over Ashley. Her faith in God grew with each word she whispered.

Tomorrow is a new day. I'll get to school and eat breakfast in the cafeteria whether Ashley wants to be friends or not. I've noticed the girls who sit alone. I'll make new friends. I'll go to volleyball practice and make new friends with girls on the team. I don't know if Ashley will be nice to me or mean. Either way, I know Elohim, Creator and Sustainer of all that exists, loves me and will help me. No one will ever make me feel thrown away again.

Sam closed the book and found his dad in the garage working on the lawn mower, "I'm finished with chapter one. Elohim, Powerful God, Creator and Sustainer of all that exists."

Dad wiped grease from his hands. "Great job. Did you notice the verses Grace's mom gave her to read? I want you to spend some time reading them. Pray and ask God to help you know him as Elohim. How will knowing Elohim help you while you adjust to your new school?"

"Well, because he created me, he understands how I feel. He will be with me and help me make new friends and, because he sustains me, I'll be fine while I wait."

"You're right, he will take care of everything."

"Thanks, Dad. I'm glad I am getting to know Elohim, Creator and Sustainer of everything that exists."

"Next Saturday. Same place, same time?"

"Same place. How about an hour later?" Sam laughed.

KNOW GOD BETTER

You read about your newest video game, study your favorite sport, practice your hobby—all so you can grow in your knowledge and perfect your skills. You don't excel by wishing, you improve because you choose to do the work. The same is true about your relationship with God. He wants you to know him better today than you did yesterday. Are you ready?

Look up the verses Grace's mom gave her. Copy the reference or the entire verse in your journal and write down what you learned about God's character.

Answer the question Sam's dad asked: How will knowing Elohim help you?

Dear God,

Thank you for creating me in your image. I want to know you better. Please help me remember you have a plan for my life and, no matter what happens today, I can trust you. There's a lot I don't understand about you or why I have sad days, but I am glad I know you love me and are always with me.

I want to remember what your name, Elohim, means. I praise you for being the Creator and Sustainer of everything!

Amen

CHAPTER THREE:
EL SHADDAI, "ALMIGHTY GOD" THE GOD OF MORE THAN ENOUGH
IIIIIIIIIIIIIIIIIIIIIIIIIIIIIIIIIIIIIIIIIIIIIIIIIIIIIIIIIIIIIIIII

Pronounced: el-shaw-DIE[3]

Sam woke up to the Saturday morning sound of neighborhood lawn mowers. Well rested from sleeping in, he decided to read before heading downstairs for breakfast.

El-Shaddai means God Almighty. El points to the power of God Himself. Shaddai means one who nourishes, supplies, and satisfies. God wants to bless you. He wants to give you all you need. He is able to give you more than enough. This name pictures God as One who is powerful enough to do just that. Only an all-powerful God can bless all mankind with all kinds of blessings.

The LORD appeared to ninety-nine-year-old Abraham and said, "I am God Almighty (El Shaddai). Live in my presence and be blameless. I will establish my covenant between me and you, and I will multiply you greatly. (Genesis 17:1-2 NIV)

---

3   Names of God, Rose Publishing 2003

God spoke to Abraham and said,

1. I am GOD ALMIGHTY, EL SHADDAI
2. I want you to have a relationship with me; choose to obey me.
3. When you walk with me and obey all that I ask of you, I will bless you with more than enough.

God's message to Abraham is for us too. When we trust and obey El Shaddai God Almighty, he will take care of our every need.

Have you ever wished you had the answers to questions such as:

Why does God allow me to hurt?

Why doesn't God stop bad things from happening?

Will my life ever be better than it is right now?

Meet El Shaddai, God Almighty, the God of More than Enough[4] of everything you need.

NOAH

"Noah, please sit down. We have something we need to tell you." Dad held one of Mom's hands. In the other, she held a tissue.

What's happened? Has grandma died? Where's my dog? Maybe that new video game I want is just too much money.

"Oh, hey, don't worry about getting me that new video game. I know money is ..." Noah tried to lighten the mood.

4   The Names of God, Ken Hemphill, Broadman and Holman, 2001, page fifty-seven

Mom spoke first, "We are not here to talk about a video game. Do you remember we prayed and asked God to show us what he wants for our family?"

Dad spoke before Noah could answer, "God has answered our prayers, Son. We are going to be a part of starting a new church."

"Awesome! Where? We could meet at the park, or in the old strip mall in one of those empty stores or even our living room."

Dad placed his hand on Noah's shoulder. "All great ideas but, no. God has another plan. Our church plant will not be in our living room or even our community. God is sending us to a new town. We'll move 1,000 miles away. I will go ahead of you and Mom so I can get everything ready. You can come for a visit when school is out for the summer."

Leave my friends? Leave my teammates? My church? My school? Leave my hometown?

He had many questions. And even more emotions.

That night, instead of sleeping, he tossed and turned. He couldn't stop the tears as his throat tightened and his stomach churned. Minutes later, he clenched his fists and punched the pillow he cried into.

Noah's dad began to pack and plan. He would need to leave soon. Noah's family prayed together and asked God to help them to trust him to provide for their many needs. Noah kept most of his thoughts to himself.

The day came when his dad had to leave and begin the work God had waiting for him. When

Noah and his mom said good-bye, Noah's throat and eyes burned. He wanted to be strong for his mom. He hugged his dad a long time, and then he went to his room.

"God, why have you done this to my family? We love you. My mom and dad have taught me to trust you. Why would you make us leave the only home I've ever known? Why would you ask my dad to go without us? Don't you know we need him around here? I don't like any part of this, God, but I love you. I want to trust you. Please help me to trust you. Please keep my dad safe. Please give Mom and me the strength to do what we need to do until our family is back together."

Noah missed his dad more each day. He struggled to concentrate at school. He prayed all the time, asking God to help him control his anger and fear. Noah thought the final month of the school year would never end.

June finally arrived and with this came the promise of being together as a family once again. Noah and his mom prepared to go visit Dad. They planned to stay a whole month. Noah's energy surged as he thought about seeing his dad and getting to be a family again.

I wonder if Dad misses me as much as I miss him? How soon will I meet other kids? Will they like me? Will there be a football team? This is going to be so weird.

The North Star shimmered and led the way as Noah and his mom began the long trip. Noah fell asleep as soon as they pulled out of the driveway.

The car stopped moving and startled Noah. He sat up. "Are we there yet?"

Mom laughed. "I hate to tell you, but we aren't even close. Let's stretch our legs and get some breakfast."

After many hours on the road, they finally arrived, and Dad greeted them with big hugs. Noah's heart pounded.

"Oh, how I've missed you!" Dad's hug calmed Noah's fears.

The family ate pizza together as Dad told them all about the new town.

"You're going to have a lot of fun while you're here, Noah. We'll go to festivals and camps and several churches so we can get to know the people in the community. There's a lake just a few miles from here. Hope you won't mind all the swimming and canoeing in your future." He reached for another slice of pizza and winked at Noah.

"Sounds like a dream summer to me." Noah imagined himself on a Jet Ski.

Noah met many people, including kids his age. His fear shrunk with each friend he made. He also learned what the saying 'time flies when you're having fun' means. He couldn't believe how quickly the fun came to an end.

The time grew close for Noah and his mom to head home. They needed to sell the house and pack all their belongings before they could complete the move and stay with Dad. Noah's eyes burned again. He hated being away from his father.

Get Off the Struggle Bus

Noah's stomach hurt when he thought of all he didn't understand about moving. Sometimes the night sounds creeped him out and he had a difficult time falling asleep without his dad in the house. His head ached from clenching his teeth. He had days when he disrespected his mom, because he didn't feel like listening to her. He hated being a boy with his family living in two places, so far apart.

"God, I learned in Sunday School that you are El Shaddai, Almighty God, and the God of More Than Enough. I need you to help me trust you to take care of my family. Please help me obey you and trust you to be the one who takes away my fears and takes care of all we need. I need your help to be able to listen to my mom, even when I am angry."

Noah experienced difficult days, but he learned that God is Almighty and really does provide more than enough. He learned to trust in God when he was afraid. He learned to obey God by obeying his mother, even when he felt like doing things his own way. God took great care of Noah and his mom. Soon the day came when he and his mom reunited with Dad in the new town. God provided Noah with many new friends. His new school even had a football team.

After his family got settled, Noah realized that he knew a little bit how Abram must have felt when God said, "Go, Abram, to a new place that I will show you." Abram learned to trust God Almighty to provide for all his needs and to bless his family through their obedience.

God has not changed. He taught Abram that he is El Shaddai, God Almighty. Thousands of years later, he taught a boy named Noah he is still The God of More Than Enough.

Sam took two steps at a time as he went downstairs to look for his dad. He wondered if his dad knew all he learned about El Shaddai.

Dad sat at the kitchen table drinking coffee and reading the Saturday morning paper.

"Hey, Dad, I sure can relate to this kid Noah. And both of us can relate to Abram."

"So, what did you learn about El Shaddai?"

Sam poured cereal into a bowl and sat down. "God showed Abram that he was in control, even when Abram didn't have all the answers. Abram always had everything he needed, and so did Noah. Even when his family was in two different places and he missed his dad. God provided everything Noah and his mom needed."

Dad smiled. "Looks like you really paid attention. How will knowing El Shaddai help you?"

"Well," Sam swallowed a bite, "God hasn't changed. Abram obeyed and trusted God. So did Noah's dad. Noah made new friends and even found a ball team that needed him. God will take care of us too. I'm going to obey El Shaddai, Almighty God, and trust him to be more than enough."

Dad folded up the paper and drank the last of his coffee. "Sam, I'm proud of you. El Shaddai will not disappoint you."

KNOW GOD BETTER

Before we can understand El Shaddai God Almighty in Genesis 17, we need to read God's promises and work in chapters 12 and 15. Note: a covenant is an agreement between two parties with the one in authority setting the terms, or making the rules.

Read Genesis 12:1-9 and Genesis 15:1-6.

What did God tell Abram to do and what did he promise he would do in exchange in Genesis 12:1-9?

Have you ever had to do anything that can compare with what God asked of Abram?

What question did Abram ask God in Genesis 15:2-3? Notice God didn't punish Abram for questioning his promise. Instead, God reassured him. What did God promise in verse 5? What was Abram's response in verse 6?

Read Genesis 17:1-8. Abram was 99 years old when God spoke to him and used his name, El Shaddai. In using this Hebrew name, God told Abram he alone is the One who is able to be more than enough. God even gave Abram a new name—Abraham. El Shaddai was able to give Abraham a son, even when Abraham and Sarah were both too old to have children. God keeps his promises.

What do you need today that only El Shaddai, the God of More than Enough, can provide? How does knowing God as Almighty, El Shaddai who provided for Abraham, help you trust him to be more than enough for you?

Shelley Pierce

Dear God,

I don't understand how you can hear my prayer or how you will answer. I wish you would stop bad things from happening, but I want to trust you to be El Shaddai, the God of More Than Enough, no matter what happens today.

Thank you for showing me how you kept your promise to Abraham and why your covenant with him is important. Help me to trust you and obey you.

Amen

CHAPTER FOUR:
ADONAI LORD
||||||||||||||||||||||||||||||||||||||||

Pronunciation ah-doe-NI[5]

Sam usually reserved Friday nights for video games, but tonight Sam decided to get a head start on reading. He thought about the long and stressful week. He ate lunch alone, had not made any friends, and imagined the puzzle piece he told his dad about growing larger.

Knowing God as Elohim, creator and sustainer eased Sam's anxiety. Knowing God as El Shaddai, the God of more than enough, helped him to think about the ways God had already taken care of him. Sam wanted life to get better, but he still struggled with feeling like a visitor at his new school.

He opened the book to read about Adonai LORD.

Adonai means LORD and is a term of great respect. When we pray to Adonai, we are saying to God "You are the creator and owner of everything. Without you there would be nothing. You are LORD over all that is[6]."

---

5   Names of God, Rose Publishing 2003
6   The Names of God, Ken Hemphill, Broadman and Holman, 2001, page twenty-two

The book of Judges helps us see the LORDship of God. The Midianites harassed the children of Israel, worse than a bully on the playground at school. God told a young man named Gideon he was going to rescue his people from the bullies. God said, "Gideon, you are going to be the one I will use to take care of this problem." Gideon worried and wondered how a little guy like himself could handle an enormous battle.

Gideon learned the battle was too big for him, but not for Adonai, LORD of all that is!

Have you ever faced a big problem? One so mountainous that you felt like Gideon and just couldn't see how you would be able win? You are not alone.

CALEB

"I will move out this weekend. I found an apartment across town. I have already paid the deposit and first month's rent. I can't live this way any longer. We'll talk with the kids before Friday."

Caleb knew he shouldn't be listening to this conversation. *Go now. Go outside, or downstairs, but get away from this door. Maybe you really didn't hear what you think you heard.*

He turned and sprinted for the backyard, the screen door slammed and bounced behind him. Caleb's stomach churned and rolled. His heart raced and his head began to spin. *Okay, so they have been fighting a lot lately. But everyone fights a lot ... don't they? Surely she didn't mean what she said. She's just hurt or angry right now. The argument will blow over. I'll keep busy until the week is over. That should be easy. If they can't "talk" with me, she can't leave.*

The next morning Caleb rolled out of bed and began his get-ready-for-school routine. He grabbed his backpack and a piece of toast and yelled for mom as he walked out the door, "I have band practice after school and then Marc and I need to work on our science fair project, if that's okay with you? I can grab supper at Marc's. I should be home by nine."

Caleb couldn't help but think of his little sister, Becca. *How can Mom even think about leaving Becca? She's not even old enough to go to school yet. Becca needs her. I need her.*

Friday evening arrived and Caleb had managed to keep himself busy and away from a conversation with his parents. He lay on his bed and tossed his baseball into the air, catching it with a *pop* in his mitt. Dad startled him by opening his door without knocking. He walked in and mom followed close behind him. Their facial expressions spoke volumes. As they sat down, Caleb sat up.

"Son, we have something to tell you."

No. Stop. If you have to talk, tell me everything will be okay.

"Your dad and I have had a lot of problems lately. We don't seem to be able to work them out. Our problems have nothing to do with you and Becca. You need to know I love you and your sister. My love for you will never change. I need some space to be able to sort all this out. I need to be able to think. I've got my own place and tonight is my last night at home." A tear glistened on mom's cheek.

No, mom ... please no ... but words just wouldn't, no, they couldn't be said. Words got all jammed up in the center of Caleb's throat. He knew he couldn't change his mom's mind, and that hurt too. So instead of speaking, he cried. He laid back down, rolled over to face the wall, and cried. His baseball fell to the floor as Mom and Dad left his room. They closed his door softly, but a heavy thud vibrated in his chest.

Caleb's mind stayed in a fog as the next few weeks crept by, filled with emptiness and sadness. The pressure inside his head built with each day that passed. Boiling, seething, hot pressure with no release. Caleb's anger simmered, not only for himself, but for Becca. She needed her mom. *How could she just leave like that? If I had been a better son, this wouldn't have happened. Why did I leave my shoes in the floor when mom asked me a hundred times to pick them up? I could have helped more too. I didn't listen like I should. Oh Mom, I'm so sorry. Please come back, I'll be good. I promise I'll be good.*

He couldn't find a reason to smile. Instead, he walked around with his jaw tight and fists clenched. He bounced from crying for no reason to wishing he could punch something. He picked on Becca and made her cry. Everything she did irritated him. He tried to control his emotions at school and church, but he continually failed.

One morning at church, he got upset and yelled at his teacher. He accused her of not caring about him and then he began to cry. All of his friends just stared at him. His teacher asked him to sit down with her in another room so they could talk. *Oh great, now what have I done? Dad is going to be so mad at me. Why can't I keep out of trouble?*

"Caleb, what was that all about? You know I love you," Mrs. Diann spoke softly.

"I don't know," Caleb didn't even try to hide the truth, "Sometimes I just think God must be mad at me. Or maybe he just doesn't like me. I don't know what I did wrong, I try to be good. I try not to cry. I don't want God mad at me."

She listened and then opened her Bible. "God loves you, Caleb. Listen to God's own words."

Caleb listened, but he didn't say much. *If God loves me, why are my parents getting a divorce? How come my dad doesn't talk to me? Why does my sister cry at night? I don't feel like God loves me.*

"If God loved me, Mrs. Diann, my mom would be home. If God loved me, I would have my family back together." There. He spoke his thoughts, but he didn't feel any better.

"Caleb, who created the world?"

"God."

"That's right. Who then, owns everything?"

"God." *This isn't helping me.*

Mrs. Diann used her you-better-pay-attention tone of voice, "You are right, God is creator and owner of everything. He is Adonai. He is LORD. He is holy and all powerful and, if he chose to, he could make your mom and dad love each other. He could make your mom move home. You need to know that as LORD of all, our Adonai has given each one of us the ability to make choices. He doesn't make any of us do anything, because he loves us too much for that. He didn't create puppets, he created people who can make choices."

"But why did my mom choose to leave?"

"I don't know. Here's what I do know--God loves you, and he loves your family. He is Adonai--owner and ruler of everything. As Adonai, he will give what you need during this terrible time. You cannot fix this problem. Instead, choose to trust Adonai, LORD. That doesn't mean your mom is coming home. Trusting Adonai means you believe he will take care of you. He is LORD, and he loves you."

"Mrs. Diann? I hurt all the time. I just don't think I can do this."

"Caleb, you remind me of Gideon. He lived in Old Testament days, and he faced a lot of tragedy. God wanted to use Gideon in a special way. Gideon argued and asked God, 'How can you use me? I am from the smallest family and I am the youngest.' God told Gideon 'I will be with you.'[7] Do you understand what that meant, Caleb?"

"I'm not sure."

"God had a purpose for Gideon's life, even though lots of people around him made terrible choices. God has a purpose for you too. Trust Adonai."

---

7   Judges chapters six through eight

They prayed together and Caleb cried again. He felt better though, because now he realized God was not mad at him. Adonai, LORD God, is creator and owner of all that is. The LORD loves him and has a purpose for him.

Caleb continued to ask God to bring his mom back home, but he also prayed and asked for strength to trust him. He even thanked God that he was not a puppet but could choose to love and serve Adonai. *Since you own all that exists Adonai, I know you will help me when I hurt. I know you have a big plan for me.*

Sam closed the book and thought about Caleb. He stared at his ceiling and thanked God for being Adonai, LORD. He realized that God is way bigger than any fear or sadness. *Gideon trusted God to help him defeat his enemies. God is big enough to take care of Caleb and Becca. Adonai owns everything, he's big enough to help me make some new friends."*

Sam fell asleep after thanking God for being LORD of all.

The next morning, Sam woke up before the sunrise.

"Whoa," Dad said as he rubbed his eyes, "I think I'm seeing things!"

"Very funny, Dad. I decided to get an early start on my Saturday chores so I can call Brendan and see if he wants to shoot some hoops. I found out this week that he lives just a couple of streets over. Dad, did you know God is Adonai LORD and everything belongs to him?"

"Ah, finished your reading already too?"

"Yupp, I plan to rely on Adonai LORD every day."

"Adonai, the owner of everything, cares enough about us to give us strength to get through the tough stuff."

"Caleb had some really tough stuff to handle. As Adonai LORD, God helped Caleb deal with his parent's separation. I also read how God was with Gideon in the Old Testament. God kept his promise to be with Gideon and help him defeat the Midianites. I decided God is big enough to help me make a new friend. That's why I am going to call Brendan."

Sam folded a pancake in half. He ate his breakfast as he walked to the laundry room to begin his chores.

KNOW GOD BETTER

You and Gideon might be more alike than you think. Let's take a closer look.

Read Judges 6:1-16.

Who was Israel's enemy (verse 1)?

List the ways they terrorized the children of Israel (verses 3-6).

What did the people do in response to their enemy (verses 2, 6)?

God heard the cries of the people. He reminded them of their disobedience and unwillingness to trust in him alone.

The Angel of the Lord appeared to Gideon and revealed God's plan. What did God call Gideon in verse 12?

Verse 15 shows us why Gideon didn't believe God could use him. Why did Gideon think he was not the man to defeat the enemy?

Have you ever felt like Gideon? Maybe even asked the same questions? God, if you are with us, why is this happening to us? God, if you love me, why do my parents fight? Why did my mom die? Why am I being bullied at school? Why do I hate the way I look? Really, our questions could never end.

Here's the most important part of Gideon's story. Read verse 14 and know that right after God declared he would go with Gideon, Gideon answered by using the name Adonai. Basically, Gideon said, "Adonai, you are the owner of everything, but I am not the man for this job."

Gideon had to learn, if he really believed God owns everything—that meant God owns him as well and God is powerful enough to take care of any problem.

You can read the rest of Gideon's story in chapters 7-8. Gideon's life shows the power of God to keep his promises.

How does knowing Adonai, Lord and owner of all, help you with your big problems?

Dear God,

Thank you for showing me how you helped Gideon. Thank you for being Adonai Lord, owner of everything.

I know you own me. I belong to you. I'm sorry I sometimes have trouble trusting you. I want to remember everything belongs to you and that means you can handle my problems. Help me to trust you to take care of me and the people I love no matter what.

Amen

CHAPTER FIVE:
EL ROI—GOD WHO SEES ME

|||||||||||||||||||||||||||||||||||||||||||||||||||||||||||||||||||||||||||

Pronunciation el ROY[8]

Sam went downstairs, expecting to see dad at the kitchen table. Instead, he found a note waiting:

Sam,

I'm sorry, buddy, but I got called in to work early this morning. Go ahead and read the next chapter, and we'll talk as soon as I get home. I'm proud of you for being willing to read and learn. Now if only you would work this hard on keeping your room clean.

Dad

Sam laughed out loud at the goofy face Dad drew on the bottom of the note.

He tossed an apple in the air, caught it, and stepped out the back door. The hammock seemed like a great place to read today.

---

8   Names of God, Rose Publishing, 2003

The name El Roi means "The God Who Sees Me."[9] The specific name El Roi is only used once in the Bible and is found in Genesis 16. However, many Scriptures verify not only the fact God sees, but he sees all, and he sees differently. 1 Samuel tells us God sees what is in the heart. We read Psalm 139 and learn God saw us before we were born. He knows where we are all the time.

In Genesis 16, we read Hagar's story. Hagar was Sarah's handmaiden. God promised Sarah he would give her a son. Sarah and Abraham were both very old and they were not patient as they waited for God to do what he promised. Sarah decided to do things her own way. She sent her handmaiden, Hagar, to stay with Abraham. Soon, Hagar learned that she was going to have a baby.

Hagar treated Sarah rudely. In return, Sarah mistreated Hagar until Hagar ran away.

An angel of the Lord came to Hagar and told her she would have a son. Hagar's response was "You are The God who sees." The angel told Hagar to go back home.

When Hagar ran away from Sarah she felt alone and sad. God reminded her that he is El Roi, The One who sees.

Have you felt like you didn't matter? Alone? Sad? Mistreated?

KAILEY

Kailey crossed her arms, squinted her eyes, and puckered her mouth. Once again, her teacher was

---

9   Names of God, Rose Publishing, 2003

so unfair. *My teacher hasn't given me a turn to take a message to the office. I asked first. She skips over me every time she needs help.* She pouted the rest of the school day.

When she got home, Kailey tossed her backpack onto the floor and paced in the bedroom she shared with three sisters. She hated seeing everyone else get to do special jobs at school. She wondered why she was always skipped. She wondered if her teacher even liked her.

Kailey has eight siblings, four older than her and four younger. That makes her a middle child. She loves her brothers and sisters, but she is convinced she is often overlooked and even forgotten.

I want my fair share of attention whether I get to hand out the snacks in Sunday School or I ride shotgun with mom to the grocery store. I WILL get what's coming to me!

Kailey got ready for school the next morning and smiled at her new-found confidence. When she got on the bus, she decided to sit in the very back. She heard a few gasps from the younger kids when she sat down. Gasps followed by whispers.

"What is she thinking?"

"Oh, I can't look."

"What a bad idea."

But today, Kailey didn't care. She sat up tall and stuck her chin out in determination. No one was going to make her move.

Next stop, Randy's house.

"Hey, kid, what do you think you're doing?" Big Randy. Football player Randy.

"I'm going to school. What does it look like I'm doing?" *Oh that was good, my voice didn't even shake. I'm not afraid of you Randy ... much.*

"Well, you better get yourself out of that seat. I think maybe you forgot that babies sit in the front of the bus." Randy seemed bigger today than yesterday.

Kailey squinted her eyes and gritted her teeth. "Fine." She moved to the middle of the bus. *That went well.*

The rest of the day Kailey elbowed to the front of the line, protested loudly when she saw someone get something she wanted, and pushed her way in on every conversation she possibly could. She didn't care when her friends frowned at her. This is the new Kailey.

When Kailey got home, she ran for the front door. She passed up her younger sisters. She smelled cookies when she pushed open the door. She hurried to be first to get one and didn't notice her toddler brother standing there with a grin on his face. Her backpack hit him and knocked him to the floor as she rushed past him. He cried. She shoved a warm cookie in her mouth.

"Hey," said Mom, "maybe you should tell your brother you're sorry."

"Eh, he's okay. He's like one of those wind-up toys, he just gets back up and keeps on going."

Mom frowned, but Kailey didn't notice. She grabbed another cookie and walked to the family room.

"Okay, scram!" she said to her little sister, Addie, "I've had a long day at school, and I'm going to watch my favorite game show. So, get out of my way."

Addie's eyebrows scrunched together, and her lip trembled. She ran out of the room with a tear running down her cheek.

Ah yes, this is working out just fine. I should have started this a long time ago.

Kailey continued to boss people, push friends around, and demand fair treatment everywhere she went. She didn't seem to notice her friends didn't want to hang out with her anymore. Her sisters and brothers stopped asking her to play games with them.

Kailey woke up to silence Saturday morning. *Where is everybody? That's strange, they usually make a lot of noise when they get up. And their beds are made? This is crazy.*

The house was quiet, even the kitchen was missing the hustle and bustle of family looking for breakfast. She got out a box of cereal and a bowl. She sat down to eat and saw the note on the table.

Kailey,

We have noticed that you're grumpy all the time. You treat your brothers and sisters as if they are an inconvenience to you. We decided to give you a day to yourself. Dad and I have taken the kids over to Grandma's. Here's a loaf of bread and peanut butter and jelly for your lunch. Call us if you need us.

Love, Mom

P.S. Maybe in the quiet of the day you will begin to clearly see all the ways God shows his love for you.

Well how cool is this? The entire house to myself for the day. I'm gonna love this!

When she finished her cereal, she decided to go to the family room. She turned the television to her favorite cartoons and settled into the chair she usually fought over with her siblings.

Sure is quiet around here.

Yup, quiet.

And boring.

Kailey went to her room to enjoy time without little sisters. When she stood up she stepped on her baby brother's favorite stuffed animal. *Aw, I wish I could play with him right now.*

She tossed the toy into the chair and headed for her room. She turned on some music and stretched out on her bed.

Yup, this is livin'. No worries.

I kinda miss those little voices.

Wow, this is going to be a long day.

She scuffed her feet across the floor as she decided to shower and get dressed for the day. The time was only 10:30.

The house is silent. Where's the noise? The laughter. Even the arguing. Why is no one telling me what to do? I'm alone. So alone. This is NOT a good day.

She stepped out the back door and curled up in the porch swing. Soon she was fast asleep.

The sound of the car door startled her. *They're finally home!*

Kailey jumped up and ran to meet them. "I thought this day would never end. I've missed you so much. I'm glad you're home."

"Did you enjoy your day?" Mom smiled.

"I was excited at first. I thought the entire day would be amazing. Not much time passed before I realized how much I love my family."

Mom took a deep breath, "I know being a part of a large family isn't easy. God created you with a great plan for your life. God sees you. He knows you. You don't need to be first in line in order for God to notice you. He is El Roi, the God who sees. Kailey, the way you have treated people is a sin."

Kailey didn't try to stop her uninvited tears. "I'm sorry, Mom. I just wanted my fair share of attention. I was tired of blending in. I didn't plan to be rude. Or sin. May I have just a few more minutes alone in our room? There's something I need to do."

"Yes, I will keep your sisters outside for a few more minutes."

Kailey went to her room, closed the door, and knelt down by her bed.

Dear God, I am sorry for being selfish. I'm sorry I take my family for granted. I'm sorry I take you for granted. Please forgive my sins and help me to be kind to people. Thank you for being El Roi, the God who sees me. You are all I need. I don't need special attention from people. I believe you see me and know me. Help me to show others your love. Help me to put others first. I praise you for being the God who sees me.

Kailey learned through a few hours by herself at home, God is the God who sees. She would never be alone. God would always love her and understand her.

Sam closed the book. The hammock swayed as he looked up. He saw small patches of blue sky through the clusters of leaves. He noticed a bird's nest in a branch way up high.

I don't know how, but I know God sees me. He even sees that bird up there sitting on her nest. I've felt alone since we moved here. Like no one cared. I've not made many new friends. I need to remember God sees me and I don't have to do this alone.

Dad wasn't home yet so Sam decided to leave him a note.

> Dad, this morning I read about El Roi the God Who sees Me. I am amazed that God created this big world and yet he still sees me. Last Saturday, I worked up the nerve to call Brendan to play ball. We hung out a lot at school this week. I wouldn't have had the guts to do that without knowing God is helping me.
>
> I learned something else today. I learned that even when I feel alone or like no one cares, El Roi sees me.
>
> Thank you for this book.
>
> I guess I'll go clean my room now.

Sam drew his own goofy face, took a deep breath, and turned to face his messy room.

KNOW GOD BETTER

We read Hagar's story in Genesis 16.

The culture in Old Testament days was very different from what we know today. Hagar was a servant to Sarai, Abram's wife.

Hagar became pregnant and Sarai was jealous because she had no children. The Bible tells us eventually Hagar ran away because Sarai mistreated her.

Read verses 6-15.

Where did the Angel of the Lord find Hagar?

What did he ask her?

The Angel of the Lord told her to go back to Sarai and then he gave her a promise. What did he promise her?

When Hagar realized God saw her, she knew God saw her hurt and would never leave her alone. God sees you, too. He isn't just watching you. He knows you and wants you to trust him to be with you.

Hagar didn't have control over her own life. When God became El Roi to her, the God who sees, she realized God would take care of her.

God is still El Roi. How does knowing God sees you help you today?

Dear God,

Thank you for telling us about Hagar and your name, El Roi. I don't like that all alone feeling. I'm glad to be reminded you are the God who sees me.

I love you, El Roi.

Amen

CHAPTER SIX

How Long?

Sam sat on the front steps. He looked around the yard and compared the sights to the yard they left behind.

Trees, grass, sidewalk, neighbors. Just like back "home."

He left a tire swing in the backyard and the bike path he had worn from hours of riding. He missed his upstairs bedroom and the view of the stars at night. He missed the familiar kitchen and knowing where his mom kept everything.

He kept in touch with his old friends by texting often, but texts didn't help him when he wished he could spend the afternoon gaming with them.

He began to wonder if he would ever think of this new place as home.

"Hey, what's on your mind?" Mom sat down next to him.

"Not much."

"Oh. Okay. You're just sitting here counting cars as they pass by?"

He rolled his eyes.

"So. What's up?"

"When will I like my new school? How much longer before I have friends? We've been here over a month and I don't fit in any better than I did the first day."

"Living here is going to get better, Sam. You need more time to adjust. Try to keep an open mind."

"Dad's book has helped. I like reading about God and learning more about him. I haven't figured out how to get what I read to make a difference in how I feel."

"Sounds to me like you need to get those words from your head into your heart."

Sam took a deep breath and exhaled slowly.

"Maybe you should pray and ask God to help move that knowledge into your heart."

"I'll try."

Mom went back into the house. Sam took another deep breath and decided he would ask God to help him. He decided he would look for reasons to like this new place.

CHAPTER SEVEN:
JEHOVAH NISSI—THE LORD IS MY BANNER

||||||||||||||||||||||||||||||||||||||||||||||||||||||||||||||||||||||||||||||||||||||||||||||||||||||

Pronounced: juh-HO-vah NEE-see[10]

Sam watched his dad adjust the weedeater engine, attempt to start the trimmer, and adjust the engine again.

"Why don't you just toss that and buy a new one?"

"Because this one can be fixed."

"I'm not sure the weedeater is worth the hassle. I'd probably lose my cool. How can you stay patient?"

"My frustration grows the longer I tinker with the engine. One thing is certain, if I quit because I'm disgusted, the weedeater will never work. If I take a deep breath and keep going, I will eventually get to finish the yardwork. Of course, you can always help me if you're bored."

"Um, that's amazing. You are focused *and* funny. I'm going to go read. I'll talk to ya later."

"If you change your mind, you know where to find me."

---

10 Names of God, Rose Publishing, 2003

War was common in Old Testament days. Traditionally, the opposing nations would each carry a tall pole with a flag on top that represented their country. All those fighting could see this flag, or banner. The banner helped them remember the reasons they fought and all they would lose if their enemies defeated them.

Jehovah Nissi is mentioned in Scripture only one time. The Israelites had just won a fierce battle against their enemy, the Amalekites. As they fought, Moses raised his arms and staff into the air as a banner to remind them to rely on God for victory over their enemy. When the battle ended, Moses built an altar upon the spot where he stood. He named the place "The Lord is My Banner."[11] He wanted the people to know that victory belonged to the Lord.

We read in Ephesians that we continue to fight battles. Our battles are not with people but with our one true enemy, the devil. God tells us to put on the full spiritual armor and be ready for battle. When we rely on God's power, we can trust him to bring victory over our enemy.

ANDY

CRASH!

Confusion overwhelmed Andy as the shame-induced nausea mixed with the adrenaline rush of power. He knew he would soon be in trouble, but all his anger seemed to crumble into little pieces as

---

11   The Names of God, Ken Hemphill, Broadman and Holman, 2001, page 106

small as the shards of blue porcelain that littered the floor. His sisters ran out the room the moment he picked up the lamp. There he stood. Alone. Surrounded by evidence of no self-control. If only he could turn back the clock just fifteen minutes, maybe he could avoid this mess.

Mom hurried into the family room just seconds after the lamp exploded, and now, time stood still. The corners of her mouth turned down and the lines etched across her forehead communicated clearly. Her heart was crushed by what he had done. She surveyed the sprawling mess, stared at Andy, and walked out of the room. Andy stood as still as a statue.

I didn't mean to do this. I didn't mean to hurt you, Mom. The girls .... they said ... they kept ... oh, does being sorry change what I've done? I have messed up big.

Mom returned with a broom and dustpan in hand. Without a word she handed them to Andy. He worked a long time to get all the glass cleaned up.

Andy went to his room and opened his bank. He counted its contents. $13.74. *That's not enough for a new lamp, but it's all I have.* He slinked down the hall to his mom's room. She sat in her chair by the window. Her Bible open in her lap, she had a tissue in her hand.

"Mom?"

"Come in."

"Mom, I'm sorry. Here. Here's all my money. Keep my allowance until there's enough for a new lamp. I will do extra work to make up for what I did. I'm sorry. I won't do this again. I promise."

"Andy, I enjoyed that lamp. But do you think the lamp is the only thing that is broken?"

"I didn't throw anything else. I promise, Mom. Just the lamp."

"I'm not talking about stuff, or anything you can touch or see. I'm talking about something more important."

Andy's face twisted. "I don't understand."

"I want you to spend some time thinking about how your angry outbursts affect your relationships. You can hurt the people who love you without ever touching us. When your anger controls you, your lack of self-control becomes a sin. And when you sin, you begin building a wall between you and God. He is not pleased when your anger controls you."

Andy hated the way he felt inside. Disappointing his mom was hard enough. Now he knew he also disappointed God. He decided to hide out in his room. *What a mess. Clothes everywhere. Toys everywhere. Not to mention the fuzzy sandwich on his dresser.*

He knew he should think about what Mom said, but he just didn't feel like thinking. He began to clean his room instead. He began by tossing the science-fair-project-worthy sandwich in the trash. He spent a long time sorting dirty clothes from clean ones. He decided to stay in his room as long as possible. He didn't want to have to be in the same room with his sisters. And he *really* didn't want to see Mom for a while. He hated the look on her face, and he knew her disappointment was his fault. Actually, his anger simmered in his heart. Not with his sisters anymore, but with himself.

Two hours later, Andy looked around his room with a touch of pride. *Good job, Andy, my boy. You sure know how to clean up a mess. Now get rid of the trash before a hazmat team needs to be called in.*

As he headed for the garage with a trash bag in hand, he heard his sisters giggling. *Stupid sisters. I would be just fine if they would just leave me alone. My problems are really all their fault. They knew better than to make me so angry. Stupid sisters.*

He dug the tips of his fingers into the palms of his hands. *Yeah. The girls made me angry and the broken lamp was their fault. And last week at school, when I pushed a desk over and had after school suspension? Well, that was Jimmy's fault. The guy is trouble. And now that I am thinking about injustice, Coach shouldn't have made me sit out of a game after I screamed at Eric. After all, Eric wasn't paying attention, and we lost the game. How come I seem to be the only one in trouble?*

He hung out in his clean room the rest of the afternoon. He stretched out on his bed, put his hands behind his head, and gave a sigh of relief. Knowing he's wasn't to blame for all this mess brought a smile to his face. Soon, he fell asleep.

When he awoke, Andy noticed it was 8:30 p.m. He had slept through supper. He slipped out of his room to head downstairs for some leftovers, but he stopped just before entering the kitchen.

His parents sat at the table talking. Their hushed voices had a serious tone.

"I just don't know what to do," said Mom.

Dad scratched his head. "We need to help Andy see that he is allowing his anger to cause him to sin, and that God provides a way for him to have self-control. I have an idea, but first we need to pray about a solution."

Andy heard his mom and dad as they prayed and asked God for wisdom to know how to teach him to control his anger before someone got hurt. He hung his head and his shoulders drooped.

Dad went to the attic and came back with a box. He called Andy and his sisters into the family room.

"Andy, Mom told me what happened today." Andy started to protest, but Dad held his hand up and gave Andy the stare. *Oh, this is serious.*

"God tells us in the Bible to 'be angry and sin not.' That means anger is an emotion given to us by God. We need to talk about the 'and sin not'. First of all, you kids need to remember that the devil is our enemy and he wants us to sin. He likes to give us plenty of opportunities to sin."

"Yeah, like Angry Andy who breaks things when he pitches a fit and ..." His little sister had the most annoying voice ever.

Dad interrupted, "Laura, making fun of your brother is also a sin. So is doing things because you know your actions make him angry." He opened his Bible and continued, "One of God's names is Jehovah Nissi. The name means The Lord is My Banner. Listen carefully. The Israelites had just won a fierce battle against their greatest enemy. Moses wanted the people to know God gave them victory. He built an altar and named this "The Lord is My Banner." The word banner symbolizes something to focus on. Our focus should always be on God. God tells us to expect battles with our enemy, the devil. He also tells us how to prepare for battle. Just as a military man or woman puts on the right uniform for battle, God has given us a spiritual uniform. Andy, come here."

Oh no, I'm in trouble now.

Dad opened the box, reached in and took out a belt. He placed the belt around Andy's waist and said, "Wear truth like a belt around your waist, son, and righteousness like armor over your chest." Dad pulled a T-shirt over Andy's head that had a breastplate painted on the front.

Dad continued as he placed sandals on Andy's feet, "Your feet sandaled with readiness to share the gospel of peace. Take the shield of faith with you so, in every situation, you will be able to put out the devils flaming arrows." Dad pulled a cardboard shield from the box and Andy took hold of the handle.

Dad placed a ball cap on his head and said, "Take the helmet of salvation and the sword of the spirit, which is God's word."

Andy waited for Dad to place a sword in his hand. *Cool! I am a scary and strong soldier, ready for a fight. Where's my sword?*

Dad handed Andy a Bible.

"A Bible? I don't understand."

"God gave us everything we need to know right here in his Word. Memorizing and quoting Scripture is more powerful than a sword."

Dad paused, looked into the eyes of each of his children, and said, "If you decide you are going to control your anger all by yourself or," as he looked at Andy's sisters, "use your own power to stop teasing your brother, you will soon find yourself back in trouble. God loves you so much he gave these instructions so you will have what you need to stand strong when tempted."

"Okay, so are you saying I need to wear this to school tomorrow?" Andy joked.

"Very funny. I need you to be serious. I'm saying that God wants you to pray and ask his help in every area of temptation. Anger doesn't have to get the best of you, Son. When you focus on Jehovah Nissi, The Lord Your Banner, he will help you make better choices."

That night, before bed, Andy thought about what happened throughout the day. He realized he had not even tried to control his anger. He also knew that when his sisters began teasing him, he had a choice to make and could have gone outside or to his room.

Andy opened his Bible and read Ephesians 6:10-18. He slipped to the floor by his bed and knelt to pray. He asked God's forgiveness for what happened that day. He began to think about the other times he had recently lost his temper. He knew he could no longer blame others for his choices. He asked God's forgiveness for these sins as well. He thanked God for helping him and for being his Jehovah-Nissi. He knew he needed to work to pay for the broken lamp.

Tomorrow will be a new day. I will put on the full armor, so I am ready for temptation. I will put my focus on Jehovah Nissi, The Lord My Banner.

The hum of the weedeater could be heard throughout the house. His dad's perseverance paid off.

I'm tempted to get a snack and watch a movie.

Sam looked out the window at his dad, swinging the weedeater from side to side with precision. Instead of looking for a snack, he grabbed two bottles of water and went out to help. After all, he knew he didn't have to give in to the temptation.

KNOW GOD BETTER

Jehovah Nissi, the Lord is My Banner.

The children of Israel witnessed the power and forgiveness of God first-hand. God used Moses to free the people from slavery to the Egyptians. Soon they began to complain. You can read about God's work in chapters 1-17 of Exodus. Notice how God revealed his power through the staff Moses carried. In the beginning the staff belonged to Moses but it soon became God's staff.

God's name, Jehovah Nissi, is only used one time in the Scripture, found in Exodus 17:15.

Read Exodus 17:8-16.

Imagine living in the days of Moses. You're in hand-to-hand combat, fighting for your land and the lives and freedom of your family. You might be afraid or tired. You might begin to lose sight of why you are fighting your enemy.

You look up to the frontline and see your nation's banner, lifted high above the battle. You have renewed energy as you focus on the reminder of God's presence and power.

What do you battle? Self-control, anger issues, being obedient to your parents, reading your Bible every day, trusting God, and telling the truth are all possibilities. God knows what struggles you have in your heart and mind. Difficulties no one else knows.

He is Jehovah Nissi, the Lord your Banner. Read the following verses and trust him to help you.

Psalm 20:5, Psalm 27:1, Psalm 34:18, Psalm 37:3, Psalm 46:1-3, Psalm 66:19-20.

Ephesians 6:10-18 tells us how to be ready for daily battles, whether they are with our own thoughts or with how other people treat us. Prepare and trust God.

Dear God,

Sometimes I do things I know I shouldn't do or I'm not very nice to people. I get discouraged because I want to do better, but I seem to mess up a lot.

I want to focus on you and remember you will help me have victory. Please help me to remember to put on the full armor I read about in Ephesians 6. Help to trust you and remember you are Jehovah Nissi, the Lord my Banner.

Amen

CHAPTER SEVEN:
Jehovah-Rapha, The Lord Who Heals

||||||||||||||||||||||||||||||||||||||||||||||||||||||||||||||||||||||||||||||||||||||||||||||||||||||||||||||||||||

Pronunciation juh-HO-vah RAH-fah[12]

Sam came home from school, dropped his backpack and plopped down on the couch. He grabbed his cell phone and checked the time. *4:13 Tuesday.*

He found the remote and scanned through the channels looking for something to watch.

Nothing.

Sam texted his dad.

"Do u care if I read before u get home 2nite?"

"Sure. NP."

"THNX. :)"

He made a detour through the kitchen, grabbed a bag of chips, and headed upstairs. He squished himself down into the beanbag chair by the window in his room and found the next chapter.

We read in Exodus 15 the history of the Children of Israel when they wandered in the wilderness for three days without water. They came to a place

---

12   Names of God, Rose Publishing, 2003

called Marah. They couldn't drink the water in Marah because the water was bitter.

The people complained to Moses and said, "Did you bring us into the dessert to die of thirst?"

Moses prayed and the Lord showed him a tree. When Moses put the tree into the water, the water became sweet. Moses told the people to be careful to listen to God's voice and to obey God's commandments. God's promised to protect the people against illness and disease as long as they kept His laws. God said, "I am Jehovah Rapha, The Lord Who Heals you."[13]

We all need healing in many ways. Sometimes we have the flu or break a bone, and we need physical healing. Other times, we are sad, or someone has hurt our feelings and we need our emotions healed. All people have sinned and need spiritual healing.

Jehovah Rapha (also spelled Rophe), the Lord Who Heals is the One who makes healing possible through Jesus, His only Son.

JAKE

Jake looked around the Intensive Care Unit family waiting room. He was surrounded by people he loved. His mom and stepdad waited out in the hall. His brother sat in a chair staring at the floor. His older sister rocked back and forth, twisting the tissue she held in her hands. His little sister kept moving from a chair to the floor and back to the chair.

13　The Names of God, Ken Hemphill, Broadman and Holman, 2001, page 94

I don't think she understands what is happening here.

His grandmother sat quietly holding hands with her parents, Jakes great-grandmother and great-grandfather. Grandmother's lips moved but no sound could be heard. He watched as a tear escaped from the corner of her eye.

Jake's granddad was in the ICU and the doctors said he could die.

Jake wasn't ready to say goodbye. He wanted to pray, but he didn't know what he should say.

"God knows what is best and we have to trust him, Jake," His grandmother whispered to him as she held his big sister.

"All to the glory of God," said Jake's great-grandfather.

All to the glory of God? How can any of this be to God's glory?

The doctor came in the room and everyone stopped talking and held their breaths.

"He is stable for the moment. We are arranging to move him to a hospital better equipped to help him. You must understand he is very sick and might not survive the transport, but we have done all we can for him here."

The doctor gave grandmother papers to sign. Then she walked out of the room.

And his family prayed for a miracle.

Waiting is never easy. When you are worried someone you love might die, waiting is even more difficult.

Jake looked around the small room. Wall-to-wall family. Great-grandparents who still loved each other. Aunts and uncles who had hurried to the hospital to be near their dad. Cousins ranging in age from teenagers down to toddling babies took their places in the hall and waiting room. And everyone was here because of granddad.

The chaplain came by. "The Emergency Medical Team is here, and everything is ready to transport Mr. Lewis."

Jake followed the family members and stood at the end of the hall, hoping to get a glimpse of Granddad as the nurses wheeled out him of the ICU into the waiting ambulance.

The family piled into several cars to make the forty-five-minute drive to the next hospital. Jake stared out the window. The night sky, veiled in a heavy fog, blanketed the car in the rain.

God, please don't let my granddad die on the way to the hospital. Please give us more time with him.

Jake's state of shock remained the rest of the week. He thought about Granddad all the time. He struggled to concentrate at school. Each day after school he went to the hospital. Each night he laid awake staring at the ceiling.

Sometimes he prayed.

Sometimes he cried.

His stomach hurt and his head ached.

Fear hovered over him like an umbrella.

One morning Jake went into the kitchen for breakfast and found his great-grandparents sitting at the table.

"Is everything okay? Where's grandma?"

"She's at the hospital. The doctors are running a few tests." said Great-Granddad.

Jake sat down.

"Can I ask you a question?"

Great-Granddad put down his coffee cup. "You know you can."

"The other day, at the hospital, you said 'All to the glory of God.' I just don't understand. How can this be for God's glory? If Granddad never comes home, if he dies, that can't bring God glory."

"God's ways are not our ways. Often times we cannot understand him. But you know, Jake, God never said we are to understand him. He said to trust him. When you truly trust him to take care of you no matter what, he will get the glory. God knows best."

"Right now, I am confused. The whole family has prayed that God would make Granddad better. He's not better. I don't believe God is listening."

"The Bible tells us that God is Jehovah Rapha, the Lord Who Heals. God heals all kinds of illness and hurts in different ways. Psalm 147:3 says he heals the brokenhearted and binds up their wounds. You just keep praying. You'll see. God is listening and he will get the glory."

"What do you mean 'in different ways'?"

"Sometimes very sick people get well and come home. Sometimes they die and their healing takes place in heaven. The Bible tells us heaven is a perfect place. No one gets sick or feels pain in heaven."

"Don't say that. I don't want to think about Granddad dying."

"Jake, trust God no matter what. Whether your granddad lives or dies, trust God to take care of him and you."

That afternoon when Jake went to the hospital he found his grandma reading in the ICU waiting room. He walked in and hugged her.

"Hey, Jake. Have you had a good day?"

"Yeah, I've been okay. How's Granddad? Any news?"

"Actually yes. The doctors took him off the machine that helped him breathe. He can whisper now. He told me he knew everyone was praying for him. He said he knew that God worked a miracle."

Jake wanted to cry again, this time happy tears. He felt so relieved.

"Did God make Granddad better?"

"Yes he did. We must remember to thank God and give him all the glory."

"All to the glory of God?"

"Exactly. All to the glory of God."

Granddad came home from the hospital after two weeks in the ICU. The family celebrated and laughed once again at his corny jokes and winks at grandma.

Jake hugged Granddad. "I was so scared. I didn't want you to die."

"Jake, God took great care of me. While I was sick, I knew I might not live. God gave me peace. I wasn't afraid. I knew God would heal me either by making me well enough to come home or by welcoming me into heaven."

"Don't say that. I don't want to hear that."

"Death is a part of life. You need to know that I am not afraid to die because Jesus is my Savior. I asked Him into my heart many years ago. There's no need to fear death."

"I'm trying to understand. I know God gets the glory whether you live or die because of Jesus."

"That's exactly right. Jehovah Rapha, the Lord Who Heals, gets the glory."

Sam put the book down and took a deep breath. He didn't like thinking about anyone he loved dying. He thought about the ways God heals. He heals sickness. He heals hurt feelings. Most of all, he gave his only Son so people can one day be in heaven with him.

God provided a tree that transformed the bitter water at Marah into sweet water. Sam knew that God could take his bitter feelings and make them sweet too.

If God can make Jake's granddad well, he can change the way I feel about my new school, all for his glory.

Sam texted his dad again.

"JEHOVAH RAPHA, the LORD WHO HEALS."

":)"

Know God Better

No one likes to get sick. We don't understand when someone we love has cancer or is in a car accident. We get confused about God's love for us when someone we love dies and we prayed for them to get well.

Read Exodus 15:22-27.

Have you ever spent time in a dessert? Scorching sun and no shade. The dessert doesn't sound very appealing.

This is where the children of Israel spent many years before they finally settled in the land God promised them. During those hard years, God showed them over and over again that he would provide.

Why couldn't the people drink the water at Marah (verse 23)?

Did the people have faith that God would make a way for them to have what they needed (verse24)?

What did God do (verses 24-25)?

How does God describe himself in verse 26?

God healed the bitter water and made the water sweet as an example of the ways he heals us. We must choose to have faith in him to take care of us, no matter how he answers our prayers.

Jehovah Rapha, the God who heals, knows what is best and heals in his own way. Sometimes that means the people in our prayers get better. Sometimes they do not get well on earth but are healed because God gives them a new body when they get to heaven. Either way, God wants us to trust him.

Dear Jehovah Rapha,

I don't know how you know what's best. I don't

understand when my prayers for people I love are not answered the way I want. I want to trust you to be the God who heals. Help my faith to grow when I question your love. Remind me you know what is best.

Thank you for healing all kinds of hurt. I want to trust you when I am worried or sad.

Thank you for loving me and creating me in your image. Thank you for being patient while I learn. I love you, Lord.

Amen

CHAPTER EIGHT:
EL ELYON THE GOD MOST HIGH

||||||||||||||||||||||||||||||||||||||||||||||||||||||||||||||||||||||||||||

Pronounced: el EL-yuhn[14]

"Sam, grab your book and let's read together today. Bring the book out to the garage. You can read out loud while I change the oil in my truck."

Sam skipped up the stairs and retrieved the book. He hoped to get to read *and* help his dad with the oil.

He opened the book and read about Sierra, the young girl with a big problem.

We read in Genesis Fourteen a great battle took place in the Valley of Siddom. Abram's nephew, Lot, was taken captive. A survivor of the battles escaped and told Abram what happened to Lot. When he learned his enemies had taken Lot, Abram and three hundred eighteen men attacked the enemy and brought Lot home. After Abram returned from defeating his enemies, King Melchizadek blessed him three times using the name El Elyon, the God Most High.[15]

---

14 Names of God, Rose Publishing, 2003

15 The Names of God, Ken Hemphill, Broadman and Holman,

God is sovereign, which means he knows and owns everything. The God Most High has the last say. No god greater than El Elyon exists.

God has the power to pull rank or overrule the messes in our lives.

El Elyon reminds us no matter how dark the night or how deep the trouble, God Most High is the final authority.

SIERRA

Ten-year-old Sierra and her little brother Isaac have the kind of family lots of kids dream of. A dad and mom and a comfortable house. Sierra is good at acting like she has no problems, but she struggles with one important thing—the truth.

"Mom, may I play some video games before supper?"

"Have you done your homework?"

"Yeah. I finished my work at school."

"Okay then, go ahead and play awhile."

Sierra smiled a secret smile. She would finish her homework before bed.

She fell asleep that night without thinking about homework. She wasn't concerned the next day either. Well, not until her teacher asked students to turn in their work.

"Mrs. Walker, I'm sorry but I'm not finished with mine. My mom wasn't feeling well last night, and she needed me to help with supper. I'm really sorry.

I tried, but I was too tired by the time I cleaned the kitchen."

"Oh, Sierra, I'm sorry your mom is sick. I'm proud of you for helping her. I'll give you until tomorrow to bring your homework in."

"Thank you. I'll finish my work. I promise."

The next day, she and her little brother, Isaac, ate Popsicles outside. She threw her wrapper and stick in the yard.

"Aren't you going to pick that up?" He looked from the wrapper to her.

"Nah. The wind will probably blow the wrapper away."

The wind didn't blow the trash away. The wrapper was right where Sierra littered when her dad got home from work.

"Hey," Dad called out to the kids. "Who left their trash in the yard"

"Not me." Sierra shook her head and tried to look innocent.

"I threw mine away." Isaac glanced at Sierra and frowned.

"Well, I doubt your mom left garbage out here. No more Popsicles until someone fesses up."

Sierra didn't care. She didn't care that Isaac was being punished too.

"Sierra, I need you to fold the towels in the dryer."

Sierra scuffed her feet at she scooted toward the laundry room. Objects in her bedroom distracted her from the towels, and she stopped to brush her doll's hair. With such pretty hair, she decided the doll should wear a new dress.

"Aren't you supposed to be doing something for Mom?" Isaac tapped his toe.

"My chores can wait."

Dad said the blessing and the family talked about their day while they ate.

"Did you get the towels folded?" Mom asked as she reached for the salt.

"Yes, ma'am. I even put them away for you."

"Good job. You went the extra mile." Dad took a bite of his potatoes.

Her little brother opened his mouth to speak.

"And Isaac helped me," she spoke before he could say anything.

His mouth snapped shut.

Isaac didn't speak to her as they loaded the dishwasher after supper.

"Hey, why are you mad? I didn't do anything to you. Come on, Isaac. Say something."

He sighed. "You are a liar. Don't put me in your lies." And he walked away.

Mom walked into Sierra's room carrying a basket full of towels.

"Don't speak. I don't understand why you lied about the towels."

"Mom, I planned ..."

"Your teacher called today and asked if I am feeling better. You're grounded for two weeks. I will have a list of chores for you to do. You will use your extra time to search your Bible and write down verses about telling the truth."

Sierra's shoulders slumped as she looked at her feet. She didn't dare protest. Instead, she folded the towels and wondered why she found lies so easy to tell.

I didn't plan to lie. I open my mouth and a lie tumbles out. I guess I have a bad habit. What's the big deal? Have my lies hurt anyone? No. Well ... at least I don't think they have. Mom is overreacting.

That weekend, Sierra decided to start looking for verses about lies and the truth by looking in the concordance of her Bible. She began looking the verses up, one by one, and was surprised to read God hates lies. She also read his word is truth, and Jesus is truth. She especially liked Ephesians Four, because the chapter said to listen to the truth and to speak the truth in love. Her verse search opened her eyes, and she began to understand how important being a person of truth is.

But, I lie easily. And often. Am I able to change?

"Hey, need some help with supper?"

"Sure. You can set the table."

Sierra worked slowly, hoping for the chance to tell her mom what she learned. She wanted to tell her mom of her fear that she wouldn't be able to change.

"You're awfully quiet. You okay?"

"Just thinking a lot. I started looking at Bible verses about lying."

"And?"

"God hates lies. He loves me, but he hates the lying tongue. I read a lot of verses about what God wants."

"And?"

"I need to tell the truth. Always."

Mom stopped working and sat down. "Come sit."

"I'm afraid."

"Why?"

"The truth is important to God. I'm just afraid ..."

"Afraid of what?"

"I don't think I can change. I think lying is too easy for me. I lie without thinking."

"Honey, I know you feel like you're in a battle you can't win. But I want you to learn God is greater than any battle we face. How about you read Genesis chapter fourteen after supper. Then we'll talk again."

"I'm don't understand how Abraham's battles are anything like my battles. Why did you tell me to read that chapter?"

"Melchizedek announced Abram as blessed by God Most High. The Hebrew name for God Most High is El Elyon. The name means God has the last say. If El Elyon caused Abram to win a battle against nations, don't you think God can help you win your battle with lies?"

"I never thought of that before. Maybe I'm not a hopeless case, after all."

Mom giggled. "Oh honey, you are far from hopeless. Don't try to break your bad habit alone. Pray and ask El ELyon to forgive you of the sin of lying and ask him to have the last word. He will help you to be mindful of the words you speak. You can either choose to lie or tell the truth."

"El Elyon. The God Most High. He will have the last word over my bad habit."

Dad sat on a stool by the workbench. "Learn anything useful?"

"I already knew lying is always a bad idea. Well, worse than a bad idea. Lying is a sin. But I didn't know El Elyon, the God Most High. God has the last word. Is that kinda like the Supreme Court? We've been learning about the court system in social studies. The Supreme Court is the highest court. What they say goes."

"That's a great analogy. Just one difference, God can even have the last say over the Supreme Court. How will El Elyon help you adjust to living in a new town?"

"I suppose, since he knows everything and has the last say, he can help me see things differently. He can help me change my attitude. If I ask, he will help me do the right thing and give this town a chance."

"Very good, Sam. Now, will you hand me that can of oil? Better yet, I'll show you where the oil belongs.

KNOW GOD BETTER

Read Genesis 14.

The battle Abram faced was overwhelming. Outnumbered, the power of his enemies appeared to be far greater than he could defeat. His nephew, Lot, had been kidnapped by the enemy and he wanted to rescue him.

Have you ever faced an overwhelming difficulty and you couldn't see a way out? Sometimes the adults in your life make decisions that are hurtful. Maybe you are the one who has made choices that back you into a corner.

God wants you to know his name, El Elyon, means he has the last say. Abram won the victory over his enemies because God won the battle.

You can trust God to help you overcome your own bad choices. You can trust God to be near when the choices of others cause you pain. He wants you know he is with you and is working, even if you don't see how he can make life better.

If you struggle with lying like Sierra in our story, take the time to read verses by going to the concordance in your Bible. Search for the words truth and lie and synonyms for each. You'll see the references to many verses that will help you know how important the truth is to God.

Dear El Elyon,

I am blessed by you, the God Most High, Creator of heaven and earth. I give praise to you, the God

Most High, because you give me victory over my struggles.

I'm thankful you have the last say. When I don't know what to do, help me to remember to pray and read my Bible. I know no god greater than you. You really are the God Most High.

Amen

CHAPTER NINE:
WHAT NOW?
IIIIIIIIIIIIIIIIIIIIIIIIIIIIIIII

"Thanks for the book, Dad. I learned a lot about God."

"I'm so glad. I hope what you've learned will help you."

"I've thought a lot about what I've learned about God. Before I read about his names, I knew he created the world, and Jesus died for my sins. Now I know he is Elohim, Creator and Sustainer of everything. I know he will keep me going, especially on my hard days.

"He is El Shaddai, God Almighty, the God with more than enough of whatever I need to take care of me while I get used to this town.

"God is Adonai LORD, and he owns everything. That means he owns me. I like knowing I belong to him."

Dad smiled. "You should keep reading about Gideon. I think you have a lot in common with him. God did some pretty big things through him when he decided to listen and obey. What about El Roi. What did you think about El Roi and Hagar?"

"El Roi, the God who sees me. Hagar had a lot of difficulties in her life. She didn't have anyone to help her and she ran away. But God let her know he would never leave her. I know God sees me and is with me.

"He is Jehovah Nissi, a banner over me to find hope in when I focus on him."

"You'll see a big difference when you focus on God and not how you're feeling. Your mom and I have to choose to focus on God, too."

"I learned he is Jehovah Rapha, the Lord who heals all sorts of hurts. I think that means he can heal me when I'm angry or sad.

"And he is El Elyon, the God Most High. He has the last say. That's pretty cool. He knows what's best for me and no one can change what God says."

"So, honestly, how are you doing? Do you feel any better now than you did before we began this reading project?"

"I don't feel like life here is normal yet. But I am getting more comfortable. I've made some friends. I know my way around school now. I know belonging is going to take time. I'll just trust God every day to be with me and to help me. Sooner or later, this place will be home."

Dad put his arm around Sam's shoulder as they walked to the house.

"God has plans for you, Sam. Big plans."

CHAPTER TEN:
I AM
||||||||||||

Yahweh Jehovah

When your parent's call you in from playing outside, do they shout, "Hey, you!" or do they call you by name? Of course, they call you by name. We can all agree, we like the sound of our own name. To call out our name means we are known.

You learned, along with our fictional character Sam, seven of the many names God gave himself. God's names reveal his character as well as his holiness. God wants nothing more than for you to know him and trust him.

God's proper name is Yahweh. This name is also translated from Hebrew as Jehovah.

In the Hebrew language, Yahweh is written with four letters—YHWH. The Hebrew scribes considered God's name so special, so holy, they would not pronounce it. As scholars translated Old Testament text, they added vowels from the name Adonai to YHWH to create the name Jehovah.[16]

16 The Names of God, Ken Hemphill, Broadman and Holman Publisher, 2001, page 64

God's name, Yahweh or Jehovah, means "I AM" or "Self-Existent One"[17].

God spoke to Moses through a burning bush (Exodus 3:14), giving Moses instructions to go to Egypt and tell the Pharaoh to release the Children of Israel from slavery. Moses asked God, "Who will I say sent me?"

God's answer? "Tell him I AM sent you." This name, Jehovah, means I will continue to be who I have always been.

What does this mean to us? What difference does knowing I AM make when we face problems in our lives that make no sense to us? Problems such as a person we love struggling with addiction, being picked on every day at school, worry about not having enough food to eat, or loneliness?

Jehovah, the great I AM, never changes. When God describes himself as the One who will always be as he has always been—he is telling us he was present before creation, he is the Creator, he is present with us today, and he will forever be.

Have you ever asked the question who created God? The answer you likely received was no one created God, he has always been.

This truth is too big for our small minds to understand.

We can trust Yahweh to be the all-powerful LORD he says he is. We can read Old Testament Scripture where God revealed himself to his people and we can know—Jehovah I AM hasn't changed.

We read about Jesus, God's perfect Son, in the New Testament and know that when we learn about

17   Names of God, Rose Publishing, 2003

Jesus we are indeed continuing to learn about Jehovah.

Jesus spoke to the people and described himself with what we know as the seven "I AM" statements. We read in the Gospel of John, Jesus said I am the bread of life, I am the light of the World, I am the door, I am the Good Shepherd, I am the resurrection and the life, I am the way, the truth and the life, and I am the vine. When Jesus referred to himself as I AM, the people knew he was saying to them, "I am the Messiah."

Read Exodus 3 and John chapters 6-15.

What difference does knowing I AM make in your relationship with God?

Perhaps the greater question is, do you have a relationship with Jesus?

DEAR FRIEND,
IIIIIIIIIIIIIIIIIIIIIIIIIIIIIIIIIIIIIIII

You read the entire book. I'm proud of you for sticking with the reading.

Even though you are finished with this book, you should know this is really just the beginning. God has many more names for himself. The New Testament contains many names for Jesus.

God will help you learn more about him. He loves you and wants to have a personal relationship with you.

The relationship begins when you realize you, like everyone else in the world, are a sinner. Sin is anything you think, say, or do that is opposite to what the Bible teaches. Sin is any behavior that doesn't please and honor God.

God made a way to erase your sin when you ask forgiveness and invite Jesus to live in your heart.

Read the following Bible verses so you can know what God says about sin and forgiveness.

Romans 3:23

Romans 6:23

Romans 5:8

Romans 10:9-10

Romans 10:13

John 3:16

Let an adult in your life know if you have questions about becoming a Christian. Talk with a parent, Sunday School teacher, or your pastor.

Remember, God always hears you when you pray. He loves you.

He is your Elohim, El Shaddai, El Roi, Adonai LORD, Jehovah Nissi, Jehovah Rapha, El Elyon, and Jehovah (Yahweh). He never changes.

Your Friend,

Shelley

ABOUT THE AUTHOR

SHELLEY PIERCE is a Director of Preschool and Children's Ministries and a grandma. She is the author of the award-winning speculative fiction middle-grade series "The Crumberry Chronicles" which includes *The Wish I Wished Last Night*, *Battles Buddies*, and *624 Juniper Street*. Shelley's first nonfiction, *Sweet Moments, Insight and Encouragement for the Pastor's Wife*, released March 2019. She has authored two picture books, both illustrated by the talented Courtney Smith, *I Know What Grandma Does While I'm Napping* and *High-water Hattie*. Shelley's work in progress is book four in the Crumberry series and a children's picture book called *Charlie and the Rose Bush*.

CHECK OUT SHELLEY PIERCE'S AWARD-WINNING FICTION SERIES

IIIIIIIIIIIIIIIIIIIIIIIIIIIIIIIIIIIIIIIIIIIIIIIIIIIIIIIIIIIIIIIIIIIIIIIII

The Crumberry Chronicles.
See what's up with twelve-year-old Jase Freeman in:

The Wish I Wished Last Night, Book One

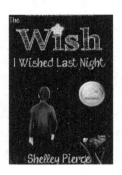

Battle Buddies, Book Two

624 Juniper Street, Book Three

Book Four in the series coming Fall, 2021

Made in the USA
Columbia, SC
11 March 2021